This vacation Bible school inspired the
Bible Buddy named Abbee.
Abbee is a bee. In God's creation,
some bees are real makers who create
beautiful pods from mud
and flower petals.

How cool is that?

Best of Buddies
I've Got This!

Written by **JEFF WHITE**   *Illustrated by* **DREW KREVI**

Copyright © 2017 Group Publishing, Inc./ISNI: 0000 0001 0362 4853
Lifetree is an imprint of Group Publishing, Inc.
group.com

Library of Congress Cataloging-in-Publications Data on file.

ISBN: 978-1-4707-4855-5 (Hard Cover)
ISBN: 978-1-4707-5021-3 (e Pub)
Printed in China. 002 CHINA 0817

10 9 8 7 6 5 4 3 2   21 20 19 18 17

I'VE GOT THIS!

Written by **JEFF WHITE**   Illustrated by **DREW KREVI**

Abbee's not the biggest
or the smallest, or the fastest
or the slowest, or the strongest
or the weakest.

But when her friends need help,
she's the first one to say…"I've got this!"

Abbee knows God made her for a reason.

Abbee's buddy Decker is making a sandcastle.

"Ugh!" Decker says.
"I can't get the windows right.
My claws are too big!"

"I've got this!" Abbee says.

She's just the right size.

"Wow!" says Decker.

"You're exactly what I needed."

"God made me for a reason," Abbee says.

Abbee's buddy Bubba
is having trouble.

"Ouch!" Bubba says.

"Something is stuck in my spout.
I can't get it out!"

"I've got this!" Abbee says,
and gives her wings a whirl.

"Thanks!" says Bubba.

"You're a lifesaver!"

"God made me for a reason!"
Abbee smiles.

Abbee's buddy Tina is building a treehouse.

"Argh!" says Tina. "I can't place the flag by myself."

"We've got this!" Abbee says.

She knows what to do.

"Hurray!" says Tina.

"I couldn't have done it without you!"

"God made me for a reason,"

Abbee says.

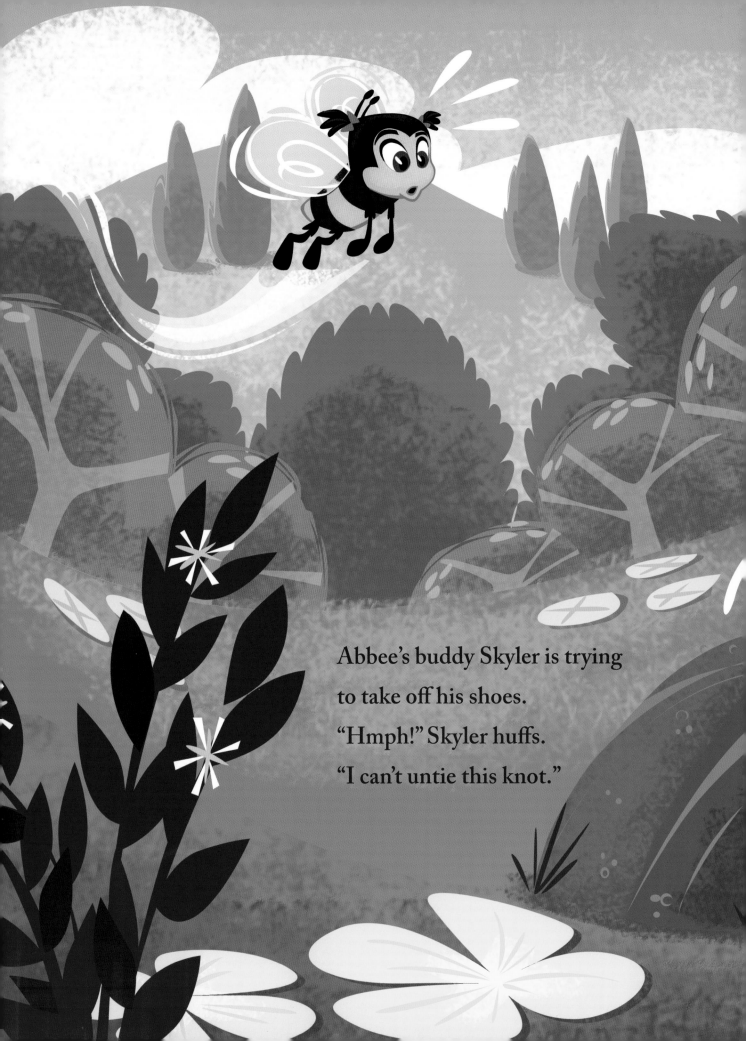

Abbee's buddy Skyler is trying
to take off his shoes.
"Hmph!" Skyler huffs.
"I can't untie this knot."

"I've got this!"
Abbee says.
She's good with
small things.

"Woo-hoo!" Skyler shouts.
"You're just the hero I needed!"

"God made me for a reason," Abbee says.

Abbee is always happy to help her friends.
And she's thankful when she says,

"God made me for LOTS of reasons..."

"And those reasons are **YOU** and **YOU** and **YOU** and **YOU!**"